OLIVER'S LOLLIPOP

Written by
Allison Wortche

Illustrated by
Andrés Landazábal

PHILOMEL BOOKS

For Ian

and for our daughters, who remind us to *look* —A.W.

To all of us who get distracted by those "lollipops" most of the time!

A nosotros los que nos distraemos por aquellas "chupetas" en la mayor parte de nuestras vidas! —A.L.

PHILOMEL BOOKS

An imprint of Penguin Random House LLC, New York

First published in the United States of America by Philomel,
an imprint of Penguin Random House LLC, 2021.

Visit us online at penguinrandomhouse.com

Library of Congress Cataloging-in-Publication Data is available.

Manufactured in China

ISBN 9780593203002

1 3 5 7 9 10 8 6 4 2

Edited by Liza Kaplan.
Design by Monique Sterling.
Text set in Chaparral.

Artwork created in gouache, watercolor and colored pencils.

When they got to the zoo, Oliver spotted it—
a huge round rainbow on a long white stick.
The perfect birthday lollipop.

"Please can I eat it now? Please?"
"After dinner, Birthday Boy,"
Daddy said.
"Let's enjoy the zoo."
Oliver held his lollipop tight.

First up: the carousel.
It spun round and round like the swirl of Oliver's lollipop.

His little brother, Louis, picked a blue beetle. Mommy rode a ladybug. Daddy got the caterpillar.

Oliver worried it would be too hard to hold on to a bug *and* his lollipop. So he waited with the stroller.

The zoo was filled with all kinds of animals.
There were **lions**. Louis ROARED with them.

There were **pandas**.
Louis *munched* with them.

There were **monkeys**. Louis
DaNCeD with them . . .

. . . while Oliver imagined how his lollipop would taste.

"Where to next?" Mommy asked. "Flamingos or peacocks?"
But Oliver wasn't really listening.

"FLAMIN

GOS!"

Louis shouted.

As they walked through the bird section, Oliver admired his lollipop's bright watermelon-y stripe.

When he held it up in the sunlight, the tiny green specks glowed.

Oliver was sure his lollipop was the most dazzling thing at the zoo.

It was almost time to leave.
Last stop: the giraffes.
Louis ran over and looked up at
their loooooooooooong necks.

Oliver looked at his lollipop.

He imagined what it would be like—
a rainbow melting on his tongue.
He couldn't wait to go home and eat it.

He pulled open a corner of the
wrapper, just to give it a sniff, when—

Oliver's lollipop was

GONE.

He hadn't even gotten one lick!
He couldn't believe it—*his beautiful birthday lollipop.*

Louis gave Oliver a hug. Daddy patted his head.
Mommy squeezed his shoulder.

But nothing helped.

As they walked back through the zoo,
Oliver's eyes were full of tears.

"Oliver," Louis whispered. "Look."

Oliver blinked—and
peeked at a toucan's beak.

WOW!

He noticed a peacock. Proud, shiny, glowing green.

He checked out the flamingos. Watermelon pink.

Oliver's eyes were wide open now.

There were **monkeys**,

and **pandas**,

and **lions**!
He couldn't decide which was his favorite.

It was starting to get dark.
But Mommy and Daddy agreed
to one last carousel ride.
Oliver chose the dragonfly.

He let go—and felt like he was flying.

When they got to the exit, they saw the lollipops again.
"Since it's your birthday . . ." Mommy smiled.

But this time, Oliver had a better idea.

And on the way home, he and Louis saw the stars.